ALOT TO SAY, SUMTHIN TO TALK ABOUT

ALOT TO SAY, SUMTHIN TO TALK ABOUT

MSCHELL

BALBOA.
PRESS
A DIVISION OF HAY HOUSE

ISBN: 978-1-4525-5765-6 (sc)
ISBN: 978-1-4525-5766-3 (e)

Balboa Press books may be ordered through booksellers or by contacting:

Balboa Press
A Division of Hay House
1663 Liberty Drive
Bloomington, IN 47403
www.balboapress.com
1-(877) 407-4847

Because of the dynamic nature of the Internet, any web addresses or
links contained in this book may have changed since publication and may
no longer be valid. The views expressed in this work are solely those
of the author and do not necessarily reflect the views of the publisher,
and the publisher hereby disclaims any responsibility for them.

The author of this book does not dispense medical advice or prescribe the use
of any technique as a form of treatment for physical, emotional, or medical
problems without the advice of a physician, either directly or indirectly. The
intent of the author is only to offer information of a general nature to help you
in your quest for emotional and spiritual well-being. In the event you use any
of the information in this book for yourself, which is your constitutional right,
the author and the publisher assume no responsibility for your actions.

Any people depicted in stock imagery provided by Thinkstock are models,
and such images are being used for illustrative purposes only.
Certain stock imagery © Thinkstock.

Printed in the United States of America

Balboa Press rev. date: 09/21/12

This book is dedicated to anyone and/or everyone who had a dream and pursued it, even when they said it couldn't be done...

And to my mom one of the strongest women I know, luv you...

REAL TALK 101...

POETRY

po·et·ry [poh-i-tree]
noun
1.
the art of rhythmical composition, written or spoken, for exciting
  pleasure by beautiful, imaginative, or elevated thoughts.

(Now with that being said, how about this)....

Someone hurt my feelings about something I wrote and they
  read
said I'm not a poet you need to find another hobby instead
So I was ready to give up and put down my paper and pen
deleted everything I wrote, went an bought some yarn and started
  knitting again
But then a good friend said I know you, you'll be back writing
  later
whoever hurt your feelings today was just being a hater.

The definition above says imaginative this means it could be true
  or false
so stop reading what other people write and trying to analyze
wonder who he's talking about or did she really just say that
elevated thoughts yep that's really deep, so criticize if u want to a
  tongue lashin is what you'll reap.
I apologize in advance for stinking up the page with negativity
I believe in keepin it real, you can ask anyone who knows me
Ok I'm done for now, that's all I have to say
thank u all for allowing me to express myself
and to the hater's...try to have yourself a nice day!

POETRY (COMMENTS)

Don't ever let someone piss on your dreams, believe in yourself,
  stay true yourself and leave no room for doubt. Real friends
  will support you and fake friends will say you cant do it
Stay away from the fake, who needs the negative energy.

LIFE

Life is only once, you cant redo it again
no retakes, erase, pause or delay
so make the most of it and live it to the fullest
wasting time or doing nothing at all is absolutely foolish
and when you've had a bad day, my advice to you would be
there's someone, somewhere much more worse off than you or me
just a friendly reminder from a friend who writes poetry
because life is universal and unsolved mystery
don't put off til tomorrow what you can do today
because your tomorrow just might be your today.

LIFE (COMMENTS)

With all the violence going on in the world, people have no
regards for human life, this is so sad...We celibrate life when
babies are born. Bottomline we only get one and
The choices you make will always affect your life, we all make
mistakes, it's ok as long as you learn from them and another
day above ground is always worth a thank you, because when
your time is up that's it, so make the most of it....

A BAD DAY

The alarm didnt buzz, i woke up late
I burnt my eggs and i dropped the plate
I chipped a nail, broke the heel on my shoe
It's monday morning already feeling blue
If this is any indication how the day's gonna be
I pity the person that messes with me

I have no money, no gas and the engine light came on
My cell needs charged and i discovered my wallet is gone
Im late for work a traffic jam and now its starting to rain
I wish i could start over and redo the morning again
Spilled coffee all over the place now the keyboard wont work
And if that aint enough, the computer screen is going biserk
I banged my knee it hurt like hell
Can it get any worse i sure cant tell
My boss called me in the office for a 30 minute chat
The end of the day, im ready to go, get outside
Guess what, my tire is flat

3 Hours later, i get home—i'm tired and ready to fight
The power is out and to top it off, now i have no light
I wrote the check, mailed it, but the payment was late
Damn can i get a break, i dont know how much more i can take
A bad day...

A BAD DAY (COMMENTS)

LAUGHING TO MYSELF BECAUSE WE'VE ALL EXPERIENCED HAVING A BAD DAY. FROM THE TIME YOU WAKE UP, ALL THROUGH THE DAY DOWN TO THE ENDING. IT SEEMS LIKE YOU JUST CANT WIN, GUESS WHAT YOU CANT. THE DAY IS STILL A BLESSING EVEN IF YOU DONT SEE IT THAT WAY AT THE TIME. I BET IF YOU LOOK BACK AT IT NOW YOU CAN LAUGH ABOUT IT.. WE'VE ALL HAD ONE...

KEEP IT 100

Folks need to say what they mean and mean what they say
it would make your life so much easier if you did it that way
stop tip towing around afraid to say how you feel
no one is a mind reader, so just say it, be the real deal
and to the recipient: Listen to what's being said, please
don't twist the words around to accommodate your needs
and to the men: we women hate when you say (I didn't say that)
because 6 months from now, we can tell you:
what you said, how you said and where you said it, when you
    said it (lol)
Just keep it 100 someone will appreciate your realness more,
    it shows your not fake
it also let's people know, you aint got the bullshit to do, some
    enemies you might make
so to anyone who's reading this, yours truly would like to say-
    -- (have a nice day)
and remember my advice friend: say what you mean and mean
    what you say.....

KEEP IT 100 (COMMENTS)

When you keep it real in all aspects of your life, everything runs much
   more smoothly also people respect you more because they already
   know you will tell it to them straight and it also shows your genuine.
I know i can respect another persons honesty, whether it's good
   or bad sometimes you need to hear the word's coming out of
   someone else's mouth
With that being said, if you speak it, own it and mean it.

A FRIENEMY
(can u relate)

A frienemy is someone close in your circle but stabs you in the
  back with a smile on their face
like having a bad day or getting sprayed with mace
will push the knife deeper just to make sure you feelin it
don't wanna see you happy, your joy tryna steal it
Can't stand to see you have anything not even a man
would steal him to, if they think they can
A frienemy can be a female or male
definitely not the one you wanna call, if you need money for bail
So people be careful who you call friend
cause a frienemy will screw you over, again and again.....

A FRIENEMY (COMMENTS)

In this case keep your enemies close and your friends closer
Not everyone is gonna be happy when you have something good
  happening in your life they will front and act like they are. It
  can be a painful realization when you make the discovery,
  because it could be a family member you consider a friend .
  Pull the knife out your back and get ghost, change your # if
  you have to, let it go and move on....

EMOTIONALLY SPEAKIN....

JIMMY'S JOINT

Jimmy's joint is a place to escape, life's never ending rat race
A revolving door of people coming and going like a shopping mall
A lifetime of memories from the pictures on the wall
Jazz music is blaring the only music allowed
No one is complaining, in fact it's very pleasing to the crowd
The food is quite tasty and always on point
The atmosphere is always uplifting in jimmy's joint
Jimmy the owner always greets you with a smile
Tell's you to have a seat and stay for awhile
Drinks are one dollar from 4:30 till 8:00
Live bands and kareoke help make jimmy's joint so great
Every now and then someone will get rowdie
Jimmy dont play that, your ass will be outie
Got the police on speed-dial the case and point
Aint gonna be startin trouble up in jimmy's joint
And if your lucky, jimmy will grace you with his base
A solo performance, all the patrons groovin in the place
And if you have a problem, jimmy's the one you can talk to
He has a hook-up for any situation and can most likely help
   you
And if he cant help you, he will find someone who can
A very friendly, caring person he is that kinda man
So when you get stressed out just visit jimmy's joint
A stress reliever that wont disappoint....

JIMMY'S JOINT (COMMENTS)

Imagine a place where you could go for a few minutes or hours just to escape the issues of the day. The music is lively, the people are friendly and the food is quite tasty. Great conversation and laughter to be had or maybe you just wanna sit and people watch or just unwind, either way it would be like a calgon moment as soon as you stepped in the door.... Take me away

PARTY OF EMOTIONS

Got invited to a party last Saturday night
Like to share some of the details if that would be alright
Welcome greeted me said hello, you can leave your coat at the
    door
walked in first thing I noticed was Happy, Joyful and Jubilant
    getting down on the dance floor
there was Lust and Passion sitting at the bar stuck together
    like crazy glue
and of course there was Sad walking around looking pitiful and
    blue
Openess walks up in the room dressed like a slut
over in the corner was Envy and Jealousy whispering about
    god knows what
Greedy and Stingy was trying to eat up all the food
I walked right pass Crazy, Insane, Stupid and Misunderstood
also forgot to tell you the 5 Senses and Curious were even
    there
the 5 Senses was telling Curious it's impolite to stare

I had a brief conversation with Truth, Honesty and Loyal they
    were really nice
Mischief is one whole hot mess, he better go somewhere with
    his devilish self
The party was going smoothly until all hell broke out, don't
    wanna miss any details
had a couple of drinks aint feeling no Pain myself...

Ok... Foolish got drunk as usual of course nobody was
    surprised
but then Sensitive got insulted and Rumor started spreading lies

Arrogant called Foolish a drunken so n so

Rage got mad screamed out real loud, who you callin a ho

what happened next you dont even wanna know, lets just say Imagination

got creative and the words started to flow

Rage slapped the crap out of Assumption, next thing you know a glass crashes

a fight breaks out, I ran got my coat cause now I'm ret to go

Helpful grabbed me by the arm and said you can leave out the door over there

in my haste to leave that's when I noticed Bashful and Shy they really make a cute pair.

Emotions are crazy they can run high or low, definitely made it one interesting night

but the best part was when Love drove me home to my Mr. Right......

PARTY OF EMOTIONS (COMMENTS)

We as human beings are very emotional people, something
hurts we cry, something funny we laugh.

We must be careful how we treat or speak to one another
because eveyone is different and what is not hurtful or
offensive to one person, could be hurtful or offensive to
another and once the words are out of your mouth, guess
what? You can't take them back....Nuff said!

HE SAID SHE SAID

He said she said are you serious
The situation is beyond being foolish and curious
We're all adults, no time for children's games
You know who you are no need to mention names
Did you check your facts or verify your info
Just ran and started gossiping the answer is no
It all starts off with, I heard or did you hear
Than you just add on to it and take it from there
She said he said, he said she said... What
He's just a bum or she's such a slut
Feelings getting hurt, people startin drama
What if this mess gets back to my mama
He said she said cuts like a knife
Doing so much damage causing scars for life
Makes you know difference cause the subject aint you
Everything else is irrevelant who cares if its true
Nice to know that the meaness is alive and well
One day karma will get you for all the lies that you tell
Dont want no parts of the he said she said game
You can just count me out and forget my name.

HE SAID SHE SAID (COMMENTS)

Some folks aint got nothing else better to do than to sit around and talk about everybodies bussiness but their own, just keep mess going. Leaving nothing but a path of destruction not realizing all the damage that's been done.
Gossiping destroys relationships and lives. Be mindful of the lies you tell, because karma has a way of catching up....

ASSUMPTION

Who you mad at, what's causing your pain
oh I see assumption got you again.

Don't you know there are 2 sides to a story
maybe you got it all wrong, the part that's one-sided
Didn't even question it just said dammit I'm done, I'm gone
now assumption got you all messed up in the game
talkin bout lose my number and forget my name

Now feelings is hurt because the person was kinda feelin you
but assumption destroyed it because that's how it do
messing up everything and have you all confused
making you feel totally used up and completely abused
well it is what it is and what will be will be
just done with the whole situation and walking away
assumption just messed you up completely!

ASSUMPTION (COMMENTS)

Have you ever got yourself all worked up because you assumed
  something? I know i'm guilty of this.
The best thing to do if you wanna know something is to just
  simply ask, sometimes you may not like the answer or you
  will discover the situation may not be nothing like what you
  were thinking—now at least you got your answer...whew
  what a relieve.

INLOVE WITH THE IDEAL OF BEING INLOVE

He's inlove with the ideal of being inlove
all messed up from a jaded past and the hurts from
yesterday.
Today your turned on, tomorrow your turned off
One day your charming and just sweet as you can be
the next, just mean and evil, straight hatin on me
I mean really who can keep up
You really dont want to be alone, but you just keep
picking the wrong one and sippin from the stupid cup
Man up and get it together and stop being the victim
women get hurt, we get over it and rise above the pain
shake it off willing to try the love thing again
you wouldn't recognize a good thing staring right in your face
it's a never ending battle never a right time or place
yep he's inlove with the ideal of being inlove
I wish you well and hope all that works out for you
because quite frankly my friend, I aint got you to do....

INLOVE WITH THE IDEAL OF BEING IN LOVE (COMMENTS)

Have you ever met someone and you felt this strong attraction, but as time goes by you end up
Discovering the person has all kinds of baggage and issues. In spite of it all you stick around only to find out (i can't do this)...Only you know how you really feel, but trust your instincts there probably right.

HAPPY THAT YOUR HAPPY

Happy that your happy living your life without me
No more arguments and drama living my life stress free
Sorry we couldnt make it, guess it wasnt met to be
Removed the shackles around my heart and now i'm completely free
Wont sing one of those who done who wrong song
Just chalk it up to the fact we just couldnt get along
Im cool with that hope you are to, wish you nothing but the best
I gave 110 percent and that you can attest
And when you really think about it, your gonna end up mad
You threw away a diamond, not realizing what you had
Its to late to reconcile because we have reached the end
But im happy that your happy and i found my smile again.

HAPPY THAT YOUR HAPPY (COMMENTS)

Have you ever been in a relationship where you were just totally unhappy, it was'nt always that way but something changed from point a to point b. So you end up just miserable and down in the dumps, for whatever reason you dont want to leave, then you ride the rollercoaster of love the ups and downs, the twist and turns, one day you wake up and decide stop let me off. Life's to short, be happy that you had sense enough to get off the ride....

SELFISH

Some people are just so selfish
it's all about me,me,me or mine, mine, mine
incapable of giving love or being loved
relationships destroyed, friendships ended
always taking but never giving
a mental dumping ground of bullshit
you get as good as you give
when's the last time you did something for someone (free)
when's the last time you gave away something (free)
your selfishness is so toxic, you could suck all the air out
of a crowded room full of people
you drain people's energy till they have no more to give
take people's kindness for granted like it's a obligation to you
NEWSFLASH: the world is not centered around you
and when your 80 years old all alone, by yourself thinking (why me)
maybe selfishness will be your friend and keep you company....

SELFISH (COMMENTS)

Its a sad state of affairs to know that their are so many people
  like this.

My mom is always telling me you gotta give or do something
  for somebody sometime and guess what, that's when you get
  a blessing. Also when you give or do something for somebody
  it makes you feel good about yourself, something so simple
  as a smile or saying hello could make someone else's day and
  the best part is.....It's free

I'M JUST SAYIN.....

A CONVERSATION WITH GRANDMA

I had a conversation with my grandma before she passed away
95 years of wisdom so she had alot to say

She said baby you's a cute gurl, how come you aint nobodies wife
man I swear you young gurls today don't know nothing about life
but grandma I said, she said be quiet gurl I'm talkin (yes, maam)
least little bump in the road you young gurls is runnin off
    and walkin
you's suppose to stick around and work it out instead of always
    leavin
I aint tellin you nothin wrong up in here this evenin

But grandma I'm tellin you, these men are really a trip
she said naw babygurl you just pickin the wrong one, see some
    things you need ta look for.
If he got 6 kids to 5 different women and runnin all over the place
run, gurl, run.... tell him to get out your face (yes,maam)

But if he's a godfearing man, goes to church on Sunday, trying
    to do right, prays daily and calls just to say goodnight
thats the one to hold on to cause he'll take care a u and treat
    you right
(yes maam)

You's a smart gurl and I know I dont need to say it
but if he already got a wife or a gurlfriend he's off limits dont
    be waistin your time with him either
you'd be in for nothing but pain and misery he's a liar and a
    cheater (grandma didnt bite her tongue) (yes maam)

If he's a dabber fella or a sportin bo, he's single for a reason,
   you gonna wanna take it slow (translation)
proceed with caution, if he look better than you or just fine as hell
because he might have sugar in his tank or he's spoiled rotten,
   got women all over the place taken care of him
then where that gone leave you (i'm just sayin).... (yes maam)

But grandma he's a badboy but a really nice person
Say what now, whatchu talkin bout
he smoke/sell them funny cigarettes what you young folks
call'em now oh yea seen it on tv... them reefers (lol)
Dont do drugs cause he gone go to jail and leave u all alone
be calling your house collect from prison runnin up ya phone
And baby I cant hep ya pay the bill with my little social security check
You might wanna leave that one alone, sound like one big
   headache. (yes maam)

But grandma he's been hurt before and now he's got issues
   about trust
oh that bullshit it's a smoke screen, if you take good care of him
   treat him right, be faithful... that hard shell will bust
And if that don't work to hell with him it's his loss go jump on
   another bus. (yes maam)

Look gurl I'm done talkin for now it's 2 o'clock I gotta go
I gotta catch that cute guy Steve Harvey on the Family Feud show
ok luv you, gave her a kiss and hug said I'll be talking to you soon
she left me last year on a cold winter day, I miss talking with her
95 years of wisdom and all she had to say!!! (smilin).

A CONVERSATION WITH GRANDMA (COMMENTS)

If you have grandparents or a grandparent still living cherish them because one day they may not be around. I was blessed to have mine around for 95 years and eventhough we had to go visit her in a nursing home i still have some great memories of her, one of my fondest is my son pushing her around in the wheelchair when he was younger, it made him feel important, oh and best believe she still looked out for me, she saved graham crackers and sodas just for me in a box she hid behind a curtain...

WRONG ONE/RIGHT ONE

Why is it that the good one is the wrong one
and the wrong one is the right one
do opposites attract is there a common denominator
do you add or subtract
Like being on the outside lookin in
or the inside looking out
pushing, pullin a tug of war jockin for position
screamin, yellin trying to drown out doubt
can't eat, can't sleep tryna stay focused on the task at hand
emotionally spent, stomach got butterflies or maybe flu-like
   symptoms
wanna run but inclined to stay dont know why it's just that way
Need a drink to calm the wicked thoughts of adult game play
Asking for nothing but wanting everything
Gonna need a ban-aide for my heart at this rate
contusions, bruises right hook to the chin took me out
Still not givin up because the wrong one is just that the wrong one
taking up space
And the good one will be there when you need them, staring
   in your face!

WRONG ONE/RIGHT ONE (COMMENTS)

Oh the war stories of the dating game..Who said good guys
finish last
Sometimes you have to deal with the wrong one first before you
can appreciate the right one or you just get so comfortable
being with the wrong one that when the right one is around
your not even perceptive enough to see it (oh, he's just a
really nice guy). To those that have their right one, your
blessed to not have to deal and to those who have not
Good luck.....

I'M JUST SAYIN

Your sadly mistaken cause your still on standby
Through no fault of your own
Your imagination has taken you off to the twilight zone
You brought the drama for no apparent reason
Just because he said hello, doesnt mean your gonna be his wife
Just because she smiled at you doesnt mean she is looking for
   a permanent hook-up for life
When your insecure you will fall for anything and some of
   everything
Starving and needy, selfish and greedy
People play games and manipulate for personal gain
Wake up and smell the coffee, dont be a victim
Stand up , grow up and man up
Dont let the situation be about them, let it be about you
Dont be a stanby be a stand out....I'm just sayin

I'M JUST SAYIN (COMMENTS)

Have you ever called someone numerous times, left messages and you never get a call back or the person answers and says let me call you back, but they never do hmmmm whats wrong with that picture. (Sounds like a standby situation)

Ladies, just because he said hello, don't go putting your wedding dress on layaway, he probably was just being friendly.

Gents, don't tell her what you think she wants to hear just to get what you want, it could backfire.....

A CHEATIN MAN
(Wow, wrote this while watching a TV show)

How you gonna slip me your number and you got a wife
who said I needed you trying to change or rearrange my life.
Do you think that little of me to approach me this way
what gave you the impression I was willing to play
I was trying to be friendly and willing to mingle
But your out here perpetrating to be single
I want my own king, be his one and only sweet thing
not just be a piece of ass or a stupid fling.

Baby where are you please find me and save me
I deserve to be happy a relationship of monogamy
a cheatin man mistress life can be very lonely I hear
what started one day turned into a year
no holidays, vacations or public outings in sight
just sneaking around and alot of lonely night
I dont need a Mr Wrong I want a Mr Right,
a good buddy a confidant a best friend for life.
Not some knucklehead with issues out here cheatin on his wife.

A CHEATIN MAN (COMMENTS)

There are single women out there all booed up with a married
  man, why?
Most likely he done fed you a crock of bullshit and you still
  hanging in there. Next thing you know years have gone by
  and guess what he's still married.
Why waste your life, he already got a wife and newsflash he
  ain't leavin her.
Stop blocking your blessings and free yourself from a dead end
  relationship
And besides if he'll cheat on her than what do you think he'll
  do to you....

I CHOOSE YOU

Your last choice is someone else's first
I choose you

Even though you beg someone else to love you
I choose you

Even though I've been hurt before dont wanna do it again
I choose you

Even though the choices you make could lead to heartbreak
or heartache
I choose you

This is one of those say what you mean, mean what you say
type of things
In the meantime just sitting back and let it marinate
and see what tommorrow brings

It might take 5 days, 6 weeks, 12 months, infinity
but the bottom line of it is, one day your first choice will be me.

I CHOOSE YOU (COMMENT)

Once you make up your mind about someone your really feelin
Let it be known and then just chill—dont be a stalker.
Sometimes the timing may not be right for that person
or they could be dealing with personal things. You've made
  them aware your job is done, if they never get back to you it
  wasnt meant to happen.

THE SOFTIER SIDE.....

PROPS OUT TO LOVE

Props go out to all the married people that have been together
for years
You found your soulmate , the love of your life, even shed some
tears
For love lost or found, enduring the stormiest of weather
But no matter what, you worked it out to keep your love
together
And even when your friends are gone, your love will be around
Safe and secure, like crazy glue, the bond is safe and sound
Secrets are kept, fights you wept, but somehow you worked
it out
The years have gone by, many in fact, that's what its all about
You've taken up permanent residence, the part that's called
the heart
A domain of love, a brick wall, let no one tear it apart
You were destined to be together so you did the marraige
thing
Not talking about shacking up , i'm talking bling a wedding
ring
Whether a private ceremony or a big bang wedding day
You guys did the damn thing and let nothing get in the way
Congratulations , may your love endure until golden age years
And help you overcome and achieve, your hope, dreams and
fears.

PROPS OUT TO LOVE (COMMENTS)

Seems like lately everyday you turn on the tv, see on the internet or hear on the radio about a high profile divorce and it aint nothing pretty. They get down and dirty. Seems like nobody wants to be together anymore. Props go out to those of you together for the long haul and making it work.

YOU ALREADY KNOW

I don't really know you, but i feel like i do
The attraction is mutual, you feel it to
Talk to you for hours and never get bored
We're on the same page my faith in love restored
The past is behind you the future looks bright
Taking it a day at a time, so far it's alright

Dont want to analyze it or compromise it
This friendship is special, it is what it is
At this rate my heart your gonna steal
Forgive me for rambling that's just how i feel
Just sit back, relax and go with the flow
I don't know why im explaining because you already know

It's driving me crazy, you're invading my thoughts
No, this is not a game concerning matters of the heart
We've already recognized that fact, from the very start
Just a friendly game of tug or war, no pressure taking it slow
But why even explain it, because you already know

It's the weirdest thing, i'm inclined to stick around
I wont run this time or completely shut down
I wont make you pay for someone else's mistakes
Going to take a chance, enjoy, whatever it takes
Now that the seed has been planted, sit back watch it grow
But why even explain, because you already know

Let's see, i'll try to explain it
It's an eight-letter word, can you name that tune
In how many notes

You run from it and crave it, all at the same time
Dont have to say it, why?
Because you already know.

(That 8 letter word is soul mate....)

YOU ALREADY KNOW (COMMENTS)

It's been explained to me, when you meet your soulmate you
just know, you don't even question it...

A GROWN WOMAN LOVE

A grown woman love is more intoxicating than a stiff drink
she'll love you when you done fucked up and cant love yourself
she'll have your back when you aint even paying attention
she's the Bonnie to your Clyde riding shotgun into the sun
she's more than a sex drive dumping ground, demanding
  respect
can't even relate to the word neglect in any shape, form or
  fashion
A grown woman is secure in herself so she don't trip off the
  dumb stuff
drama free, stress free, no time for the bullshit life is hard enough
just trying to maintain, willing to share the ride of life, but not
afraid to go it alone
A grown woman love you don't take for granted, she'll leave your ass
so fast, you'll be assed out, left scratching your head, saying
  damn what
just happened......

A GROWN WOMAN LOVE (COMMENTS)

Grown women display the same characteristics, they are confident and comfortable with them selves, you never see them sweat anything, their demeanor is just cool, calm and collected but on the flipside you dont want to rub them the wrong way or all the cool goes right out the window..

I WANT

i
i want
i want you
i want you to
i want you to give
i want you to give me
i want you to give me back
i want you to give me back my
i want you to give me back my heart
You stole it from me when I wasnt lookin!

I need my heart to live, like you need air to breath
but your doing it all for me I'm scared it's like a total
out of body experience, now I see what they mean when they
   say two hearts beat as one.....

I WANT (COMMENTS)

Have you ever been in love, i mean really in love? It is totally
crazy how you feel you get butterflies in your stomach
whenever you talk about that person, you get
Tongue-tied or you break out in a sweat whenever that person
is around, it's definately a scary feeling to let someone in
your heart, but so worth it when the
Feelings are mutual....

A RAINY DAY

There's something very sensual about a rainy day
I'd take the day off to chill with my boo and past the time away
First things first: I hope he can hook it up, because I'm not
  getting out this bed.
Yep he sure did: some coffee, eggs & toast, fruit and a rose
by the way about the rose, did I mention it was red....

So now let's see no phone, no kids, just me, my boo and this bed
Nope we cant be reached right now, please leave a message
  instead
Crack open the window, so we can hear the raindrops hit the
  ground
that's the music of love we will need as we go round for
  round
(make love, watch a movie, make love, make a movie, did I
  mention
make love, watch a movie).....

The things that would go down on this day, would put a Zane
  novel to shame,
because it's all about a grown folks day, yes the neighbors
  would know his name.
Yep, there's something very sensual about a rainy day
I'd take the day off to chill with my boo and past the time way!!

A RAINY DAY (COMMENTS)

A rainy day usually makes you lazy and because it's so yuky outside you rather just stay in. What better way than to spend the day chillin with someone special.

TWENTY-FOUR SEVEN LOVE.....

SINGLE WOMAN INDEPENDENT MOM

Mortgage, water bill, sewer bill, car note, light bill
Insurance premiums, cable, cell phone... The plate is full
No time for drag arounds, couch potatoes or bring me downs
If you cant enhance me, you cant romance me
24/7 On the grind, survival is the name of the game
Trying to maintain, 2 setbacks for every gain
Damn, can i get a break, shufflin, hustlin, scufflin
A job with benefits, a life which is stable
So tell me mr man, you know my story, what can you bring to
the table?

There's football, baseball, basketball and band—school play
choir practice, hairs cuts and doctor appointments
You gotta be: chef, maid, seamstress, doctor, play mate, mommy,
daddy, taxi, teacher, atm (can i get a dollar), protector...
A full time job with no pay, you cant call off sick or have a bad day
You are always on call and expected to be available to fill any
role in a moments notice..Yes it's alot but so rewarding
Its very hard to let someone in and disrupt what you got going on
Because you work so hard to keep it all running smoothly
Putting all your wants and needs on hold, so you can have
enough energy to pull double duty and make sure your
children are not unruly.

SINGLE WOMAN INDEPENDENT MOM (COMMENTS)

Being a single mother is hard work, sometimes it all seems so overwhelming.

Especially when you have to work for a living and maintain a household. Its a never ending rat race to a unobtainable finish line or like riding a never ending rollocoaster, alot of ups and downs, twist and turns, swerves and curves.

You just prepare for the ride and go!!! If your a praying person you already know god will pull you through the worst of times or sends little angels your way with blessings right when you need them!

YOUR A MOM NOW

Responsible for another life, this is some serious business
You've crossed over to mommyhood welcome to the club
We've paid our dues, did our time now you gotta do yours
A high school dropout not gonna cut it
Unemployed are you serious , you got diaper duty and bottles
  to make
This aint babydolls , jumprope or playing with your easy bake
Mom and dad gonna hold your down for a minute
But your a mom now so be in it to win it
So strive to be the best mommy you can be
Because you have gifted the world with a little mini-me
It's a never ending job are you up to the task
No instruction book, no manual sometimes you just have to ask
Alot of trial and error and mistakes will be made
Your the mom now, no more cookies and kool-aid
No trophies will be given at the end of the day
Your job is forever no raises no pay
So get down to business no foolin around
Woman up, because your a mom now

YOU'RE A MOM NOW (COMMENTS)

Being a mother is the most rewarding experience in life. However it is not the easiest life experience. You give up so much of yourself and sometimes you have to put your dreams and goals on hold. The baby didnt ask to be here, it was a gift.

As a responsible parent it is your obligation to be obligated, motivated and dedicated to the human life you have been gifted.

Good luck, prayers and blessings to you all , enjoy your little package sent from

Heaven....

A STRANGER IN MY HOUSE

Someone please tell me, who's this stranger in my house
he's 13, taller than me and used be quiet as a mouse
now he eat's up all the food, drinks up all the milk
say's mom can we go to the store, there's nothing in here to
    eat
I'm stunned because he said it to me in his Barry White voice
you know the one that's really DDDEEEEEPPPP.

Yes I got me a stranger livin up in my house
he said ma your butt looks big in those jeans and why you
    wearin that blouse
so opinionated and knows about everything still not a man yet
    because he's only 13.
Man let me tell you I'm not liking the teenage years
I want my baby boy back when all I had to worry about was him
    fallin down the stairs.

Dont get me wrong I love my stranger to death
someone call 911 because some of the things he says just takes
    away my breath.
I can't imagine my life without him being in my life
I'll probably cry like hell, when my stranger grows up, moves
    out and finds himself a wife
and has some little strangers to I can't wait for the day you call
    me up to tell me what your stanger said to you
because I'm gonna laugh hard as hell, so suck it up..because
    not long ago remember you was a stranger to.

A STRANGER IN MY HOUSE (COMMENTS)

We loved it when are children were babies, everything they did was so cute and when they slept they looked like little angels, enjoy your babies now because they grow up. Terrible 2's has nothing on the tween years, it's alot going on and you end up looking at your child like who is this person and even though you dont recognize them, love them regardless and hope like hell you dont catch a case!

(Wrote this one for my son, hugs and kisses...Love you, mom)!

THE KIDS TODAY DON'T KNOW

The kids today don't know the kids of yesterday
There was no ipad, xbox, computer or playstation
We made up games and used are imagination
We'd play outside from sun up till sun down
Always something to do, no time to mope around
We had: jacks, jumprope, tag, flag football, hopscotch
We rode bikes for hours, shoveled snow for money, babysitting
    was a business.

We respected are elders, said yes maam and yes sir
Mr and mrs. You got permisson to do things, like eat at someone
    else's house or spend the night . We didn't have cellphones
    but you knew to be home before the street lights came on

There was no time out, you got laid out or knocked out if you
    wanted to act out and lets not forget about getting your own
    switch.

Mcdonalds was a special treat, you ate whatever was cooked
    or put on your plate, dont like it dont eat
Obesity was never an issue because your parents always had
    stuff for you to do before you got your me time
And they only asked you to do something once.

THE KIDS TODAY DON'T KNOW (COMMENTS)

I hope this one makes you smile as you think about your childhood and remember the innocence and good times!

The world today is such a different place, the kid's today are forced to deal with issues the kids of yesterday could'nt imagine , won't elaborate just take a look around......

REFLECTIONS....

MISS YOU FOREVER

The day you left was the saddest day ever
I cried and cried why, forget about you never
I just couldnt believe it, devastation set in
To know that i would never speak to you again
You cant make a phone call, you cant send a text
I cant go on without you, have no idea what comes next
Please someone help me, sometimes the pain is so bad
Missing you like crazy, feeling angry, sad and mad
Because you had to leave me, i cant seem to get it together
I'll always keep you near, because the memories last forever
Wish we had more time together before you had to leave
I love you and i miss you, this you can always believe
Guess i better go now, had a few things i wanted to say
Just wanted you to know that i was thinking of you today
So R.I.P dear loved one, your an angel now with wings
I know your watching over me and doing angel things
I'll see you on the other side one day, in a different place
And when i get there i'll be looking for your smiling face.
But until that time comes, forget about you never
Just know this one thing i miss you forever

MISS YOU FOREVER (COMMENTS)

Death is final, there's no coming back. When you loose a loved one it's a pain that never completely goes away, but as times goes on it gets to be a little bit easier to deal with. Sometimes when people pass unexpectantly, it leaves a big question mark "why" or you wish you could have said something or did something differently. That's why you need to show your love, give your flowers while the person is still alive. None of us are guaranteed another day above ground.

Please stop the violence that's someone's child gunned down like an animal while your sitting in a jail cell, that mother will suffer a devasting loss for the rest of her life and saying i'm sorry cant bring back her child.

SOULTRAIN IN HEAVEN

Man did you know they are jammin up in heaven
the Soul Train left today to many names to mention
ok I'll name a few anyway.

There's Whitney, Etta, Vesta, Amy, Heavy D, Tina Marie
Luther, Teddy, Gerald, Rick James, Barry White
2pac, Aaliyah, Left Eye, Biggie, George Howard,
Grover Washington, Wayman Tisdale, Miles Davis, Marvin
    Gaye
Ray Charles, James Brown and I can't leave out Michael
Ok I'm done someone else help me out, I think I reached my goal
Yep they jammin up in heaven
Looking down at earth wishing us all LOVE, PEACE and
    SOOOOOUUUUUL......muah
(r.i.p Don Corenlius)

SOUL TRAIN IN HEAVEN (COMMENTS)

This poem was inspired by the death of don cornelius

Soul train was one of my favorite tv shows as a teenager. Saturday morning 10 oclock. You couldnt wait to see who the guest were going to be, you got to see the latest fashion and the hottest dances and you heard the latest songs and of course my favorites were the scabble board and the soul train line.
I still like to watch the reruns today, the music still sounds good and even some of the fashion has come back around. This show touched so many lives on so many levels in so many ways, i say thank you for the memories and the experience.

SPEAK ON IT......

SHE'S THRIFTY

She's thrifty, didnt know you could do so much with a
10 Dollar bill
On a first name bases with the employees at
The salvation army, the thrift store and the goodwill
Can work miracles with a can of beans,carrots,rice and
A crockpot
Sittin back chillin with a five dollar ceiling fan when
Its hot
Can work a discount, sale or a coupon....Get the item for free
Finding a 20 dollar bill is reason for a shopping spree
Tuesdays is senior day, Wednesday is 50 percent off day
Thursday is a day of rest, payday Friday is a call off work shop day.
Will google a yard sale and be there before dawn
Buy patio furniture and a mower for the lawn
Home before 10 for a litte snack and some rest
Gotta get ready for Sunday to show off their best
Having a thrifty friend is a blessing indeed
Can go in their basement and find what you need

THE STATUS OF ME

Why are you so worried about the status of me
When you see me on the street you dont even speak
My number didnt change have you called it
When you had me you didnt know how to treat me
When i was a friend you talked behind my back
When i did my best it wasnt good enough
When i was there through thick and thin, you proved you didn't
    know how to be a friend
When i was struggling did you offer to help
When you needed shelter i gave you a key
Now you wanna know about the status of me

Well i couldnt be better, my status is good
You changed the rules in a game I chose not to play
Thats what makes it so easy to walk away
I forgive you but i will never forget
Your so yesterday, as i move forward without regret
I wish you well in all that you do
But trust and believe, im no longer concerned about
The status of you......

THE STATUS OF ME (COMMENTS)

In life friendships are made, relationships develop . You never completely know a person and just when you think you do, life throws you a curveball to show you.

It can be so disappointing for someone to let you down and they dont even see or acknowledge what they did. Thats when its time to let go and walk away if you know you didnt do anything to that person you can walk around guilt free.

If a person did you dirty, they dont deserve a space or place in your life. Let them be on the outside looking in... #ICULQQKIN

THE END

Once you've reached the end there is no more
You cant go back and get a refill
So if you done than be done
It's reached the end my friend bye bye, be gone
You cant negotiate or manipulate it to your favor
Because the end is the end is the end
See when you've reached the end, if you turn around and come
    back it's still the end
Wake up and realize when you've reached your end
Stop walking on egg shells, tiptoe-ing around it
Acting as if everything is okay, that's just rubbish
That's like saying, the nerdiest of nerds is thuggish
Once again, if you done than be done
It may be the end but actually the beginning
A new game being played and so far your winning
A fresh start, a new page, old baggage checked at the door
Yesterdays misery is forever no more
So when you get fed up, just finished my friend
All i can tell you is the end is the end.

,

THE END (COMMENTS)

Don't waist your precious time in a dead end relationship
Whether it's a love interest, a frienship or a dead end job
People will come and go, life is to short and tommorrow is not
   a guarantee. Get rid of the baggage, drop the dead weight
   it's time to rejuvinate and elevate to the next level.
Good luck with that.....

NOBODY CAN BE YOU

Nobody can be you better than you, you dont have to act there's only one you walking the earth, when you were created there was only one of you made. No imitation or recreation of you, what you see is what you get. So be the best you can be, be a you somebody else would wanna be. Be good to yourself, be true to yourself, be you and stay you at all times, dont change you to fit into somebody else's space, life or world if you have to change then that's not the true you. Your responsible for you, so own up to the mistakes you make, keep it real dont be a fake

Watch the roads in life you take and be careful of the friends you make.

Nobody can be you better than you, when you look in a mirror

The person looking back is who...You!

BE
U

Hope you enjoyed this book as I've enjoyed writing it. Book 2 is in the making. Stay tuned......

CPSIA information can be obtained at www.ICGtesting.com
Printed in the USA
BVOW04s1854160314

347708BV00001B/88/P